+100

Young Authors

of

...hree

1990

YOUNG
AUTHORS
OF
AMERICA

☆

VOLUME THREE

1990

Edited and With an Introduction by
Ellen Rudin

Published by
The Trumpet Club
666 Fifth Avenue
New York, New York 10103

ISBN: 0-440-84465-7

Printed in the United States of America
January 1991

10 9 8 7 6 5 4 3 2 1
OPM

CONTENTS

INTRODUCTION

Why does someone write a story or a poem? One answer is for self-expression. Another is the wish to communicate thoughts and feelings. Some people write because they want to amuse others or to entertain them. Whatever their reasons, more than 7,500 boys and girls wrote works and entered this year's contest.

For the judges it was a rich feast. The metaphor is apt—a huge smorgasbord of ingredients, shaped by individual skills into unusual delights. This is the Young Authors of America Contest's third year, and by now certain themes are familiar: families in all their variety, friends in all of theirs, school, pets, sports, vacations, holidays (Christmas is number one, with Halloween and Thanksgiving Day close behind). Mysteries, fantasies, and ghost stories are favorite forms. Examining the self; relating to others; coping with loss, doubt, failure; hoping, dreaming, achieving triumph—young authors, like grown-up authors, struggle to make sense of life and death; and they do so with curiosity, passion, humor, and clear eyes.

This year, as in previous years, first, second, and third place winners were chosen, and they are published in full here, along with seven runners-up. As the judges read, many poems began to stand out. Poems of eighteen young poets were selected as winners and comprise, for the first time, a special poetry winners section in the book. In addition, the work of eighty-one children received honorable mention in the contest and their names appear at the end of the book.

And what an exciting collection of writing this book is! Malathi Sundaresan's "A Dream Come True" tells how a young boy's love for and faith in his astronaut father, lost on a space mission, mysteriously influences the father's safe return. "The Living Doll" by Jenny Dunning hilariously treats the plight of a hapless fifth-grader pursued by three classmates who all want to marry him. The title character, nerdy but likable, of "Levente" by Levente Fulop is such a model student that he is incapable of giving a wrong answer, no matter how desperately he tries. Becky Jantz writes in "Fang" about an unwanted blind puppy who, with the help of the boy who loves him, learns to lead a normal life; and in "Oh, Annie" by Brooke Homyak, a big sister realizes with a sudden pang how much her little sister means to her. A talking dog gives birth to an unusual litter in Stacy Whetzel's "The Dog Who Could Talk." The first-person narrator of "Friends—Who Needs Them???" by Brenda Diaz slowly arrives at the painful answer she has known all along. "Rex on the Road" by Schuyler Merker Pisha tells about a boy (not a dog) who leaves home for a while to get perspective on his life. Kevin Crook's eerie "Just a Guy on a Field" touches on the very meaning of existence. And in "The Computer and the Mouse" by Miranda Beames, a girl who will do anything to win the class presidency finds she has gone too far. The poetry winners—21 poems by 18 writers —capture a powerfully touching range of personal experiences and observations.

Why does someone write a story or a poem? A child sent a letter with her manuscript. "When I grow up I would love to be a writer," the letter said. "I feel grand just by sending my story to you. Even if I don't win best story I feel one step closer to my chosen career."

A teacher sent a letter also, saying every child should be thanked for trying. To each boy and girl who entered this year's contest, congratulations. Whether or not you were a winner, you have shown you can write. If you want to stay a writer when you grow up, keep writing, keep trying.

ELLEN RUDIN
August 1990

A DREAM COME TRUE

by
Malathi Sundaresan

1

Jeff slammed the door behind him and fell across his bed. "He just doesn't understand! That makes me so angry!" Jeff howled. Suddenly his door opened and his mother was standing there, hands on her hips, and looking a little upset. She started to say his name, but instead she sighed.

"You've got to understand that Richard isn't used to being a father. Though I know we are not married yet, he is still trying his best," his mother said.

"You want me to understand!" Jeff said. "He doesn't even know how to treat a future stepson! He doesn't know how long it has been since I've had a father. The worst part is that just because I like space stuff he thinks I am a fool!"

"I know that Richard doesn't understand that you have a wonderful imagination, but I do," his mother said.

Jeff sat up. "He is not my stepfather yet, and I hate to tell you this, Mom, but I really don't want him to be. And, Mom, you know it's not just my 'imagination.' I'm interested in space because of Dad."

"I know, dear. You are the only person I can talk to about your father's disappearance, but you have to try to let go, a little at least. I am still very happy that you're keeping a part of your father around us."

They were both silent for a while, thinking. "Well," said his mother at last, "I'll try to talk to Richard. And, Jeff, before you go to bed, tell Richard good-night. You know, whenever he visits, you never say good-bye. He is about to leave for his apartment now, so come and tell him good-night," his mother said.

She gave him a kiss on the cheek, and left the room.

Jeff blew his hair out of his eyes and fell back on his bouncy bed. He lay there thinking about his father and how it had all happened. Then he got up and reached for his journal. There was a bookmark in the page that he always read to remember his father. He turned to the page and took out the bookmark. Jeff whispered to himself, "I have read this so many times I probably know it by heart." He turned on his lamp. Then he took a breath and started to read what had happened three years ago.

Nine days ago from today, March 26, 1982, the worst thing in the world happened to me and my mom.

The day of March 17, 1982 started out wonderfully. My dad was about to go on his first mission in space. Since it was St. Patrick's Day and my dad was wearing white, I gave him a little pinch, a great big hug, and I told him good luck. My mom did the same, except she gave him a kiss. We waved at him until he was in the shuttle. We all watched the shuttle blast off.

It was wonderful. The sight was just amazing. We watched it soar higher and higher until we could no longer see it. After about five minutes everyone left, either back to their homes or to tour the space center. Mom and I went into the space center and talked to many of the people involved with the flight. Our conversation was interrupted by a man who had a message from the mission control room. His voice was quick as he said this: "We've been having great contact with the astronauts, but the bad news is that all of a sudden there was a disturbance and we were disconnected."

We ran down the hall with a couple of other men. We reached the control room and one man said, "Ma'am I'm sorry, but no one else is allowed in this room." My mother's face looked terrible, and it was turning a little pale. She put her head against the glass window where she could see what was going on. I held her hand and I also tried to see what was going on. It was hopeless, though, because we couldn't hear anything. Then a man in a black suit came out and said, "We're not sure, but we think that the shuttle was hit by an asteroid. We think it has gone off course. I'm afraid we will be unable to communicate with them until they get back on course."

"What if they don't?" my mom said with a little fright.

"Well, chances are that they will get back on course, unless they are damaged severely." He looked at Mom's face, full of shock, and his expression changed. It changed from a worried look to a sympathetic look, and then he said, "Don't worry. You just go home and rest. If anything changes, you'll be the next one to know. Don't worry; we'll contact you soon."

So we went home. Mom was very depressed, and didn't say a word about what had happened. I, on the other hand, had one-million things racing in my mind at once. I was a bit scared for both my father and mother. My mom was driving, you know, and she wasn't paying much attention to the road. I noticed how her mind just wandered off once in a while. Well anyway we got home. Mom slumped on the couch and I went straight to my room. Later she came in and talked with me about what had happened that day.

The next morning Mom called the space center. When she got off the phone I could see tears starting to form. She told me that Dad was not found, and that they had no idea where to locate them. After Mom said this in a quivering voice, she burst into tears. I hugged her and she just put her head down.

A long time later she stopped crying and came to my room. She cuddled me up like a little baby. I didn't mind because I was upset and her love and warmth was what I needed. She talked to me a little and then we sat there listening to the silence.

Today was the ninth day since Dad's disappearance. This is the day I started writing in my journal.

Jeff held the book in his hands and his eyes were on the page but his mind was far away. After a while he turned to the next entry.

Sorry I haven't been writing in here, Journal. Days have gone by and Mom is still depressed. Even months have gone by. Today is October 27. But this afternoon Mom realized that she had to go on with life. Well, everything is starting to get back to normal. Except one thing. Deep inside of us, our hearts are still holding on to Dad. We have too much love for him to let go.

There was one more entry. Jeff kept reading.

Today is July 16, 1985. It has been three years since Dad's disappearance. Now Mom is thinking of marrying again. The man's name is Richard and he's not very nice. He comes over once in a while for dinner, and sometimes they go out to dinner. Though he doesn't come over often he can see that all my interests have to do with space. Richard thinks I go too far. O.K., maybe pretending that my forks and knives are space shuttles is a little strange, but the word he called me was absolutely terrible. He called me a fool about my imagination. He doesn't know that he's calling my dad a fool too. My love for space is mostly because of my father. I don't see how he can't understand that.

Jeff slowly closed his notebook and looked around his room. He looked at all of his space shuttle models and all of his space posters. Then he put his head down. He lifted his head and looked at the time. It was time for him to go to bed. He changed into his pajamas and went under the covers. The blanket made him feel warm and cozy. Jeff realized that he had forgotten to brush his teeth and decided he would do it in the morning as usual. He didn't want to get out of his cozy bed. It was so comfortable that he soon fell asleep.

2

Jeff woke up to find himself floating. He was wearing a huge astronaut outfit. He rubbed his eyes and tried to look around. There was almost total darkness. Then he heard a strange voice, mechanical like a robot's voice. A faint figure appeared out of nowhere. The figure opened its mouthlike opening and said, "What are you doing here, and who are you, and what do you want?" He was fairly short and was a bluish-green color.

Jeff was about to answer his questions when another voice, from behind him, said, "Move out of the way." The new stranger walked up to the alien and spoke to it. "You said you wouldn't hurt anyone, especially children." Then he turned around and looked into Jeff's face. "Where did you come from, young man?" he asked.

Jeff suddenly realized that he couldn't breathe. His heart stopped, his eyes enlarged, and his hair stood on end. The stranger's face was so familiar that he thought it was his father. He hadn't seen him for three years but he knew it was his father.

"Jeff?" said the stranger.

When Jeff slowly nodded the stranger grabbed him towards his chest. Now Jeff was positive that this man was his father. He couldn't believe it. In that moment he felt his heart start again and he began to breathe.

They were distracted by the words of the alien: "I tell you, sir, I had no intention of hurting the boy. I was just asking questions." Jeff's father looked at the alien and frowned. His expression

changed when he looked at his son. Without saying a word, he put his arms around Jeff's shoul-
ders and led him away.

As they walked, his father talked to him. "I am
so happy you are here, son," he said. "But let me
just tell you one thing about those aliens: Stay
away from them. They might be dangerous. We
have been watching them for a while now. Luckily, I found you in time. We are not sure if they are
friendly, because when we arrived they weren't
very welcoming."

Jeff's father stopped and looked at him. A smile
came over his face and he gave Jeff a big hug.

After they had walked about a mile and a half,
Jeff spotted something glowing white.

"What's that?" he asked his father.

"It's our space shuttle," his father replied. "After it was hit by the asteroid, we had to get it to
safety. So Larry, our commander, set course for
the nearest safe landing. We think we are on
Phobos, a moon of Mars."

Mars, thought Jeff.

"We are doubtful, though, about the atmosphere
here. We have found out that we are able to
breathe this air—that's how we have been alive for
these past few years—but we could be taking a
chance. We don't know what effect this atmosphere will have on our bodies. It may be too late
for us because we have already been exposed to
the air, but you still have a chance. Don't ever stop
using your oxygen supply unit until it runs out.
Do you understand?"

"Yes, sir, I understand." Jeff stopped for a second to think and said, "Dad, I have a question. Have you tried a scientific way to find out if the air is dangerous?"

"We've done what we can to test it. Well, forget about it. Just keep your space suit on," his father said. They were almost at the shuttle now. Jeff slowed down and said, "Dad, are we going to get home?"

His father looked at him a long while before answering. "Well, you see, our landing wasn't too smooth. So when we hit the surface, our mission specialist got a bad hit on the head. In fact it was so hard he had amnesia. He still can't remember much."

When Jeff heard this he was shocked.

His father continued. "So far we haven't been able to fix the shuttle. We are starting to lose hope."

Then his father saw the look on Jeff's face and his tone of voice changed. "Don't worry, son. Your dad's here. I won't let anything happen to you."

"Dad, I am scared. What can we do?" Jeff said.

"We are doing all the things that we know. We just don't have the intelligence of our mission specialist."

Jeff waited and then said carefully, "You know, Dad, maybe I can help. A trained mission specialist gave me private lessons in mechanical engineering. I took those lessons for two years after you left. I guess I did it because of you."

"Son, this is important. You are only a boy."

"Dad, I may be able to do something. Let me try," Jeff pleaded.

"Well, O.K. But be careful, and tell me what you are going to do before you do it," his father said.

They went inside the shuttle. Jeff's father introduced him to all of the station operators, and then he told them about his son's idea.

Jeff looked at the damaged controls. He closed his eyes and tried to remember what his teacher had taught him. Then he opened his eyes, explained his plans to his father, and then his hands went to work.

His father hadn't thought that Jeff could do anything to help, but now he began to have hope. Jeff worked for more than two hours, with his father's supervision, before he stopped and said, "This is all that I have learned. Let's just hope it works."

While the commander examined the controls, Jeff's father reminded him, "Even if the boy did fix it, our wing is still damaged."

Then the commander said, "We'll get to that. For now, I have to finish up on the control box. Let me tell you that your son has done a great job."

But Jeff was watching the commander. "Did I do something wrong, sir?" he asked. "I mean, you are still trying to fix it."

"No, no, you were a great help, and you even pointed out the problem, perhaps without knowing it. But it still doesn't seem to be working correctly. Let me see what I can do now. You can be proud of yourself, Jeff." He winked at Jeff and then he got back to his work.

"I'll see what can be done about the wing," Jeff's father said. As Jeff and his father walked out of the shuttle, Jeff's father told him how impressed he was with Jeff's skill. "I'm proud of you, son," he added. Jeff felt proud, too, and his face wore a huge smile.

Then his father said, "Do you have any ideas for fixing the wing?"

"Not really, Dad. We need a helpful tool that could straighten out the wing. Or if there is a possible way to replace the missing parts of the wing that have broken off, that might help," Jeff said.

"Well, we probably have a tool that can change the wing's bent position and its dents. I'm not sure about the missing parts, though. I do have an idea, but I doubt it will work."

"What's that?" asked Jeff.

"My plan is that if we look for something half the mass of the undamaged wing, and fix it onto the damaged wing, we could have equal mass right there. That way we can chunk off the bent part of the damaged wing. It may not take us too far but that is the only idea I have. If we're desperate enough we can try it."

"Well, Dad, aren't we desperate?" Jeff said.

"You're right, son. Let's go!" his father said.

They explained their idea to the other crew members. Everyone agreed that it was a good plan, maybe not the best, but they didn't have any other. Joe and Angela, the other crew members, and Larry, the commander, stayed in the shuttle, but Don came to give some help. Jeff; his father; and Don, the copilot, all set out for a hard day's work.

Hours passed. The three men were exhausted and they all sat down. They had accomplished their job. They weren't sure if it would work, but they had to try. They were too tired to try it out right then, so they decided to sleep first, and then they would be ready.

Jeff's father and Don awakened first, and the crew began to make preparations to leave Phobos. They let Jeff sleep. In the three days since his arrival he had worked as hard as any of them—and harder than some.

Thirty minutes before lift-off the commander decided to free Joe, the mission specialist, from where he was confined. They had tied him up because after he got amnesia, and found out that he wasn't on earth, he got a little rowdy. At first he didn't understand, and afterwards he fainted. When he regained consciousness, he almost went crazy. Now he watched them quietly.

The rest of the time before lift-off was used to double-check all of the equipment and the mechanical functions. They also used some of their time to get ready. All of their possessions were packed up, so they had nothing to worry about. Except one thing: The fact that the shuttle might not fly was a big worry. What kept them going were their faith and their hope.

Everyone was prepared. They all waited, except Jeff, who was still asleep. It was then ten minutes till lift-off. The time was passing by quickly. It was already four minutes before lift-off. Then it was three, then two, then one minute. The commander quietly started the countdown. In the near-silence all they could hear was the soft breathing of Jeff.

Then as the commander counted down the last ten seconds his voice grew louder. "Five . . . four . . . three . . . two . . . one . . . LIFT-OFF!" With a roar, the shuttle shot into space. The crew held their breath until they knew it was safe. When they all knew it was safe, they cheered in happiness. They were floating in space. The commander located Earth and then said, "Crew, we're going home."

Jeff woke up and saw that he wasn't in the shuttle anymore. A light was flickering. His eyes adjusted to the darkness and then he saw his space shuttle models. He looked at where he was sitting and he saw his teddy bear, his blanket, and himself sitting on his bed. He got up and looked in the mirror. His forehead was full of perspiration, his palms were sweating, and his heart was beating very fast. He turned on his lamp and then he looked around. He was in his room. He couldn't believe it. He had had a dream. It was impossible for it to have been a dream because it was so real, Jeff thought. Suddenly he felt someone embrace him. "You've been asleep for one whole day," his mother said. "I was so worried."

Then Jeff said, "Mom, you'll never believe this. Dad is going to be O.K." She reached over to Jeff's television, which was flickering, and turned up the sound. "I know," said his mother. "I left you for just a moment to get my glasses. Look what is on the television," she said excitedly.

Jeff turned around to see an airport runway on the screen. A newscaster was talking with high spirits. Jeff understood what was happening and his eyes enlarged. He turned to his mom and then back to the television. He couldn't believe it. His dream had come true!

After the shuttle landed, Jeff and his mother jumped in the car and went to the space center. They both knew that none of the crew members would return home until after a long period of debriefing, but Jeff's mother still stepped on the gas. When they arrived at the space center, they jumped right out of the car. They ran to the front office and explained who they were and whom they wanted to see. The cheery man who was at the front office led them to another man who could help them out even more. He recognized who they were and said, "My guess is that you two are anxious to see Thomas. Well, we'll get him back home as soon as possible. They've been gone for so long that they will have to stay in quarantine for more than two days. The maximum time you will have to wait will be a week."

"Is there any possible way I can see him sooner?" Jeff's mother said.

"No, I don't believe so. Don't worry, ma'am. We'll call you and tell you the exact time he will arrive. We sent all of the other astronauts' friends, relatives and families back to their homes with the same information as we gave you. Don't worry; we'll call you."

With that they both decided they had no choice but to go home. They were disappointed but they were happy.

In the car Jeff's mother asked him the big question he wasn't sure he could answer. "Jeff, how could you have known that your father was going to be safe before you saw the television?"

Jeff tried to find a reasonable answer and then he said, "Well, Mom, it's a long story."

To his surprise she took his answer and forgot all about what they had just said. "I'm so happy that your father is back," she said. "When I first looked at the television I was shocked. Now I am overjoyed."

"I know how you feel, Mom. I feel the same way."

After a while Jeff noticed his mother thinking with a smile on her face. Then she started crying in joy and said, "It's been so long I didn't think he would ever come back. This is the happiest day of my life."

Jeff could feel the happiness. The smile on his face went from one ear to the other. That was his only way to express his wonderful feeling inside. He felt like rainbows of joy were going through him. He felt excited and happy all at once. He didn't want to wait a week to see his father, but he knew that he must wait. Jeff thought about how happy his family would be when his father came home. He thought about how his father might look. Then he thought about Richard and said, "Mom, what are we going to do about Richard?"

His mother laughed at first but then became serious. "I don't know. I guess I'll call him and tell him what happened. He'll understand."

They turned into their driveway. The second they went into the house, Jeff's mother picked up the phone. She dialed Richard's number and waited. After about four rings Richard picked up the phone. Jeff's mom told him what had happened. She also told him that because her husband came back she wouldn't be able to marry him.

Jeff was surprised that Richard said that he was happy for her. He was even more surprised that Richard said he would like to meet Jeff's dad. Jeff knew that Richard was probably sad and so did his mother because she said, "I'm not sure but I think he might have taken it pretty hard. He handled it well, though. I'm glad he wants to meet your dad. When he said that it made me feel that he understood."

"You know, maybe Richard isn't a bad guy," Jeff admitted. "Even so, I'm sure glad that Dad is back."

3

There was only one more day until Jeff's father would come home. Jeff and his mother were too excited to finish the lunar module model that they had been working on all week. All they could do was watch TV. Even that didn't get the homecoming off their minds. So they agreed to just get some sleep because in the morning they had to wake up early.

In the morning they got up and got ready. They left in a hurry because of their excitement. When they got to the airport they looked everywhere for Jeff's father. Suddenly Jeff was startled by his mother's voice.

"Thomas!" she yelled. Jeff ran after his mother

and then he saw the man he had been wanting to see. His father was standing there, with his gear beside him, and his arms around his wife.

Jeff ran up to his father and hugged him tight. They all were crying with joy. Jeff felt that this moment was a moment that he wouldn't forget. Then his father lifted him up and gave him a big hug. He set him down and then they all started to walk towards the car. Jeff and his father carried the luggage while his mother uncontrollably talked. Jeff felt left out, but when they got to the car his father gave Jeff the most attention.

Jeff couldn't believe what was happening. His father was actually home. He felt bursts of joy among his family. Even when they got home the joy was not gone. Jeff thought it would never end. He even wished that it would never end. This was Jeff's happiest moment in his life.

Hours later they finally calmed down. Jeff and his father talked to each other like they had never talked before. Jeff felt like crying. His father said the most comforting words—how much he loved him and how much he had missed him. His words were all Jeff wanted to hear. It was so special to hear these words from his father. He felt the same way his father felt about him. They talked about almost everything until it was time for dinner.

When the food was on the table, they all sat down and said their prayers. Jeff and his family said a long, beautiful prayer, and then they started to eat. They barely touched their food because they were so excited. They talked throughout the dinner, and Jeff's father told them what had happened.

"You two know that we were hit by an asteroid, right? Well, after we were hit we landed on this sort of planet. We still don't know where we were but the people at the space center are trying to find out. We knew we had to get off that place but we couldn't fix the shuttle. After two years we decided to quit. We didn't have any hope. Then something told us that we could do it, so we tried it again. This time we tried harder than ever. We wouldn't let anything stop us. We all worked hard but our mission specialist worked harder. We were all amazed by the fine work our mission specialist did. We owe him a lot. With his talented work our space shuttle was able to fly. You know, the thing that kept me going was my loving family. I worked my tail off because I wanted to be with my family again."

Jeff's father paused and said, "The funny thing was that we felt like someone was there with us." When he said that Jeff almost spit out his water. Then his father said, "If God hadn't given me the hope and strength I probably wouldn't have made it. God also gave me two other things that helped me through this whole mission. He gave me you two. Your love was in my heart every second," he said with a smile.

4

It has been a month since Jeff's father returned. Everything is getting back to normal. His dad isn't planning to go back up in space for a while. Right now, in fact, his father is in the hospital for tests, because the air he had breathed during the years in space might have harmed his body. But the doctors think the air will have only a little effect on his lungs. His mother is much happier now and his father is now good friends with Richard. Everyone is happier than ever, and Jeff is especially happy because he just turned into a teenager. Now Jeff has a happy ending to his three journal entries having to do with his father's disappearance.

Tonight he read his first three entries to himself and then he started writing his fourth entry.

> Today is December 6, 1985. My father has been found. The day he came home was the best day in my life. I've never had a better day. Well, one day was almost as good as that day. It was the day I turned 13. That day was yesterday, December 5. I'm finally a teenager.
>
> There is one important thing I would like to write. The day my dad arrived on Earth, I had just dreamt that my father would be all right. I was in the dream and I helped save him. I feel that the coincidence is rather strange, that my dream had actually come true. The important thing is that my father is back.

Jeff closed his journal and then put his pen on his desk. He thought that maybe because he was becoming older he wouldn't need a journal anymore. He thought about it for a little while and then decided that he didn't mind having a journal. With that, he picked up his pen and opened his journal. Then he wrote his last words for the day.

He wrote this: Maybe dreams really can come true.

THE LIVING DOLL

by
Jenny Dunning

September 3

I just moved to Chicago. I don't think I like it here. It is too big. On the way here my one-month-old baby brother stunk up the whole car and we had to wait almost an hour until we saw a rest-room break. We started on our way again and when we got to Chicago I about fainted. The buildings were huge. My dad is a doctor, and that is why we moved here. Dad says he can make more money. My mom said that she wouldn't get a job for a while because she just had the baby.

When we got to the apartment, I thought we could have gotten a much nicer one than this. My mom liked everything but the kitchen. She said it was too small. She said that Dad should take down a wall and make a bigger kitchen. I thought we should give me a bigger bedroom because mine is tiny. I just hope that the school is small because I hate being lost. But from the looks of this city, it will be huge like all the rest of this city. Oh well, I have to go one day or another, so I guess I better go tomorrow.

September 4

This school is huge! I don't want to go here. When I went into the room there were about 40 kids in there and a very pretty teacher. She asked, "Young man, are you lost?"

I said, "No."

She asked, "Are you a fifth-grader?"

I said, "Yes."

"Did they tell you a number in the office?"

"Three."

"Well, that number," she explained, "means you're supposed to be on the third floor."

I asked, "Why can't I be in this class?" I didn't want her to think I was pushy but I was so scared of going anywhere else and getting lost.

"There is no more room. We have 39 kids in here."

"Wouldn't it be better if you had 40? Then you could put people in groups of 10. That would be much better than having people being left out, wouldn't it?"

She smiled and said, "Yes."

"Well, then can I stay?"

The teacher paused for a moment and then said, "Sure. I will go to the office and tell them."

I think I am in love with the teacher.

When she came back she had a chair and someone brought in a desk. She moved the desk by a girl. On the front of her desk was the name Holly. The girl told me to go to the teacher's desk to get some paper to make a name tag. When I brought it back, the girl said, "Hi, my name is Holly. What's yours?"

"Kyle," I replied.

Then she asked if I needed any help coloring my name tag. I told her I didn't care, so she pulled her chair next to mine.

A little while later it was time for recess. I went outside and Holly grabbed my arm. She walked me over to two other girls and said, "Kyle, this is Amy and Suzi." I looked at them and said, "Hi"; then I looked at Holly and her hand, which was still on my arm. I guess it was nice for her to hold my arm since I was new and all. Besides, she was kind of cute.

"Holly," I said.

"What's wrong, Kyle?" she asked, still holding on to my arm.

I chickened out. "Oh, nothing." I stood there while she was talking to her friends and her hand was still on my arm. I didn't know if I should grab her hand or put my arm around her, or if I should say anything at all.

Finally the teacher blew the whistle. We all lined up and went inside. I looked at Holly, and she kept winking at me, so I turned around. Then I looked over at Amy and she seemed to be staring at me. Then I looked at Suzi and she also looked like she was in a daze staring at me.

September 5

The next day I walked into the classroom and there was a piece of paper on my desk. I went over and opened it.

> *You're invited to a wild, fun party!*
> *Holly Brown is having a party at 3:45*
> *after school tomorrow. We will be*
> *playing games and eating cake and*
> *drinking pop to celebrate her birthday.*

I looked on some of the kids' desks with invitations, and they were all girls. How could I go to a birthday party with all girls?

When everyone came in they started singing "Happy Birthday" to Holly. She sat down at her desk. The teacher asked Holly what she was going to do for her birthday.

"I'm having a bunch of friends come over to my house for pizza, cake, ice cream, and pop. And we're going to play lots of games."

"Sounds like fun," the teacher said. "Who is invited?"

"All the girls," Holly said. "And maybe, um, maybe some other friend." Then she looked over at me, but I had sunk down in my seat about three feet. Then Holly added, "But you guys would not know him. He is from another town."

"What's his name?"

"Kyle," Holly answered and then stammered, "No, I mean Mike. Mike Brown, my dad's brother's son."

"You should bring him to school to visit. That would be great for all of us to meet him."

"I don't think he can come. He, um, is sick."

"But if he is sick," the teacher asked, "then how is he going to make it to your birthday party?"

"Oh, well, he will be better tomorrow. He just has a headache."

I stared up at the teacher. She knew. I knew she knew. I just hoped no one else would find out.

September 6

The next day after school, we went to Holly's house and ate and drank pop. Then it was time for her to open her presents. Amy had gotten her a horn for her bike; Suzi's present was a big hat with bananas, apples, carrots, cherries, and leaves all over it. I was beginning to worry over what I had gotten her. I hadn't known what to get her, and I wanted to get her something I thought she'd like. If I thought she'd have been happy with a bike horn, I would have gladly switched presents, but it was too late.

She opened mine. I got her a ring with two fake pearls and a fake diamond on a fake gold band. She loved it. She started jumping up and down screaming, "I'm engaged! I'm finally engaged!"

I looked at her like she was crazy. She came up to me and gave me a big kiss and a hug, and all of a sudden I had the feeling my insides were going to come out.

She ran in the kitchen and told her mom. I saw her mom coming out to the living room, so I ran into the bathroom and locked the door. Holly's mother knocked on the door, but I wouldn't answer. She said I could come out because everyone was outside. I opened the door, and Holly's mother began talking, and everything she said sounded like she was planning our whole future together. She said that we were too young to get married and that we should wait until we were 18. I tried to tell her my side of the story—that I would be friends with Holly, but not marry her. I said that the ring was just a birthday present, not an engagement ring. Holly's mom didn't think that just being friends was a good idea after giving her a ring. She looked really hurt over what I said. I didn't know if she was kidding around, because you never really know what's going on inside the mind of a grown-up.

September 7

The next day at school Holly was running around the school telling everyone that we were engaged. She even showed our teacher! The teacher started to laugh but then said the ring was beautiful. Then Holly showed the whole class and said that it had two real diamonds and two real pearls and a real gold band.

September 12

That week the ring was all she talked about. Then one day I saw her in the park. She was crying. I went over and asked her what was wrong. She said, "How come you never invite me over to your house to eat since we are almost married? Maybe I should come over tonight and tell them the good news."

"What good news?" I asked.

"You'll find out at supper tonight at your house."

That night before she came over I told my mom the story. She thought it was silly, but she said if Holly was taking it seriously, I should too.

When Holly came over she had this little seat like my brother's little seat that we have in the car. She had a blanket over it, and she sat down at the table.

"What is in the seat?" I asked. "Why did you bring the seat?"

"This is the surprise," she answered. "Kyle, you're a father."

"When did you have a baby?" I asked, shocked.

"Yesterday," she answered. She pulled the blanket off the seat. It was a doll.

"You had a doll?"

"No, this is our son, William."

"How could you name a doll William?" I shouted. "How come I never got to help name him?" Suddenly I realized what I was saying. That I wanted to name a doll! Why would I want to name a doll?

"It's not a doll; it's our son. Don't call our son a doll."

September 13

The next day at school she brought the stupid kid or doll or whatever it was. She told everyone it was our son. I ran outside the room because everyone was teasing me. The teacher came out in the hall, and the only thing she told me was I would have to work this problem out myself.

During lunch I walked over by Holly. I didn't want to break her heart, but I didn't want to be a father either. She was feeding the doll, and when she saw me she said, "Good, now you can feed the baby. I haven't gotten to talk to my friends all day." She handed me the doll, and I did the only thing I could think to do. I threw it on the ground. She ran over to it and started bawling. I immediately felt bad that I had done it.

She ran to the teacher yelling, "Call an ambulance!" The teacher asked why and Holly said, "Kyle murdered our child!"

I ran over to Holly and told her that I didn't want to be a father. "I have more than 20 years to be a father—or even older!"

She ignored me and shouted, "You probably killed him!"

I went over and picked up the doll. Its head had fallen off. I didn't know if I should laugh or cry. I started laughing. I wondered if I would get sent to the principal's office for this. I figured I'd probably get locked in the closet for doll abuse.

Holly came over to me and said, "I told you that you had to learn to be a father, but, no, you wouldn't listen. Now I know that I won't let you hold the next one because I had another one yesterday." Then she grabbed William and said, "Lucky for you, the head pops back on." Then she made me promise I would not hurt him again.

September 17

The next day she brought William and our new baby daughter, Sally. She made me hold William while she took Sally. Over the next few days things only got worse, and before I knew it we had 12 kids, but she got baby-sitters for them. I really thought this was getting out of hand, because she had two big dolls named Raggie and Andy, and they were as tall as her.

One night Mom and Dad asked if I had gotten the doll mess straightened out, and I told them I couldn't.

September 18

The next day at school, Suzi came up to me. She had a doll in her hand. I didn't recognize this one, and I was afraid Holly had had another one. But it was worse. Suzi handed it to me and said, "You are a proud father to our baby boy."

Amy was right behind her and she also handed me a doll. Then Holly came up and they all started arguing about who was the father of what baby. I didn't know what to do.

Amy said, "Let's let him decide who he wants to be married to and whose kid he wants to be a father to."

They all stared at me, and Holly shouted, "I married him before any of you! He gave me a ring, and he would never leave me with 13 kids."

"Thirteen kids?" I asked. "I thought you only had 12."

"There will be 13 as soon as I make more money."

"More money?" Amy said. "You mean you buy your babies?"

"No," Holly insisted.

"Well, then what do you mean by making more money?"

"It costs a lot to be treated good in the hospital. And it costs to buy them food and get a good baby-sitter at home." Then she turned her attention to me and asked, "Well, Kyle, who is it going to be? Who are you going to pick—me, Amy, or Suzi?"

What could I say? I was trapped. "I, uh, I pick . . ." Suddenly the bell for school rang, and I took off for class, leaving the three girls standing outside.

*　　　*　　　*

Boy, was I lucky, because I had no idea who I was going to pick. I guess I did marry Holly first, but she had too many kids. I would marry Suzi, but she talks too much, and when she starts to talk it never ends. I would marry Amy, but I didn't like her pigtails.

September 19

Today the teacher announced a talent show at school. All the girls had to do something together and all the boys had to do something. The girls wanted to have a beauty contest, and I was chosen to be a judge. During class Suzi threw a piece of paper in my direction. It landed between my desk and Fred Zuberman's desk, the bully of the class. I started to reach for the note, but Fred put his foot on it. At the same time, the teacher noticed and walked over to the note. She made Fred lift his foot, and she saw my name on the note.

"Kyle, is this yours?"

"Yes, it is mine. It's a list of homework I needed

to get done." She picked up the note, and I thought she would open it, but she handed it back to me.

"That's a good idea, Kyle," she told me as she walked back to the front of the room.

Quickly I opened the note.

> *Dear Kyle,*
>   *We are writing this letter because we want to know who you really like. So when the beauty contest is over whoever wins will get to marry you and you will have to give that person a kiss.*
>
>> *Your lovers,*
>> *Holly, Amy, Suzi*

At lunch Amy sat down beside me, Suzi sat on the other side of me, and Holly sat across from me. All the boys started calling me a sissy. When I finished lunch, Holly took my tray, and when we were getting ready for recess, Amy gave me my coat and Suzi gave me my hat.

Later on, the teacher announced that she didn't think a beauty contest was a good idea for a talent show. I was glad because I wouldn't have to choose any of the girls. When I came in from afternoon recess there was another note on my desk.

> *Dear Kyle,*
>   *Today after school you have to choose who you want for your wife.*
>
>> *Your true lovers always,*
>> *Holly, Amy, Suzi*

When I read the note, the only thing I could think was I had to hide somewhere. Just before school let out, I went up to the teacher and asked to go to the bathroom. She said school was almost out, but I told her I didn't think I could hold it, and she let me go. I ran straight home.

I went to my room to write a note for the girls. My room was a real mess, so I grabbed a piece of paper and went into my dad's den to get a pencil. I decided I needed somewhere completely private to write this note, so I went into my mom and dad's room. They have a closet above their bed. I got on top of the headboard and opened the latch on the door and climbed in. I left the door open slightly so I could get back out when I finished.

I was reaching for the light when I heard my mom coming up the stairs. She had my baby brother and started changing his diaper. She must have noticed the door was open because she shut it. I was about ready to scream, but I didn't know how much trouble I'd get into for being in there in the first place, so I waited for her to leave and then turned on the light inside the closet. I got as comfortable as I could, and then I started to write.

> *Dear Holly, Amy, and Suzi,*
> *I have decided who I want to be with. It is none of you. You always fight over me, so why go out with any of you? I will still be your friend, but not any of your husbands.*
>
> *From*
> *Kyle*

After I finished writing the letter, I tried to get out, but Mom had latched the door. I yelled but it was no use. I figured I would have to wait until someone came back upstairs. I sat back and started looking at some of the boxes stored in the closet. I decided to open up the box I was sitting on. It had some old clothes and hats. Then I pulled out a dusty old photo album. I started to flip through the pages. I didn't recognize anybody, because the pictures were so old.

I was about to put the album away when one picture caught my eye. This picture had a wagon with two big horses and an old lady and a little boy and some old man on the side of the wagon. I sat and looked at it for a long time, but I didn't know who it was. I looked in the box and it had the clothes that were in the picture. Underneath those clothes was another framed picture. This picture had a boy who looked like me and he was holding some dolls in his hand. In fact, there were three dolls. I was confused. And then I was scared.

I started to bang on the door of the closet. Finally Mom heard me and ran up the stairs and opened the door. I started talking so fast Mom never heard anything I was trying to say.

She helped me down and asked me why I was up there. I held out the picture and asked, "Who is this, Mom? And why is he holding dolls?"

"Oh my," Mom said. "I had forgotten all about this picture. This is my dad. Your grandfather."

"Grandpa played with dolls?" I asked, shocked.

"No," Mom explained. "The funniest thing that happened to him when he was little was these three girls that liked him, and they all wanted him to be the father of some dolls. One day all the girls got together and had Grandpa's dad take a picture of him holding the dolls. They all got a picture to keep and after that they left him alone."

I didn't know what to say. Grandpa had been dead for two years, and I missed him so much. I never would have thought that, even though he was gone, he would still be able to get me out of any mess I might get into.

I smiled. And then I laughed. I held the picture close to me. Suddenly it seemed as though I had no problems at all.

LEVENTE

by
Levente Fulop

Levente had big eyeglasses. He had ash-brown hair and had a little body and long legs and was 5'7" (because of his legs). Yes, you might think he is weird and is a nerd by the way he looks. Well, you're right; he is considered a nerd at H.B. Lee Middle School. Levente didn't care about how the other boys teased him; he didn't care what the girls called him. In fact, he didn't even notice them; at least he tried not to.

Levente had a problem: He was the smartest student at H.B. Lee and always got straight A's, or a 4.0. He had been getting those grades ever since he started kindergarten and he didn't like that; he hated it. Once he tried getting a question wrong, but it just wouldn't work. He couldn't think of anything else but the right answer. Mrs. Carlson (his teacher) seemed to notice that and kept saying after each right answer Levente got, "I like how smart Levente is. I wish you were all just like him. All you have to do is say the right answer to my questions."

Whenever Levente heard her say that, he would scowl at her (because he had been hearing that for the past seven years he had been in school). One day he asked, "How come you never make any remarks about the other kids except me and Jeremy?" Jeremy was just about, but not quite, as smart as Levente was, and whenever Levente wasn't in the classroom because he was doing algebra (calculus), Jeremy would take over and say the right answers, and he hated the good remarks and grades he got just as much as Levente did.

"Well, because you and Jeremy are the only ones who get all of the answers right to my questions or to the homework I give you," was Mrs. Carlson's answer.

Levente and Jeremy looked at each other worriedly. "I wish I'd get a worse grade than A or A-plus," said Levente.

"Same here," said Jeremy.

Then the lunch bell rang. Levente sighed, went to his locker, which was filled with citizenship stickers, honor roll stickers (of course), spirit stickers, student-of-the-month stickers, on time, attendance, and all other kinds of stickers. Levente opened his locker, took out his lunch, and stood there wondering for a moment about how he would try to get a problem wrong. It seemed impossible to him, but with a little effort, he could probably manage to get at least one wrong.

"Come on!" said Luke (his best friend), interrupting Levente's thoughts. "We'll be late for lunch!" Luke took off running, motioning for Levente to run too, but no matter how hard Levente tried, he could never run. It was against the rules and he couldn't do anything wrong. Now just as he was going to break loose from the rules, and began to run. Luke came walking slowly back, head down, and swearing between his gritted teeth. Luke was always getting caught running in the halls and had to walk back to where he started from, and then walk to where he was going.

"Nice try," said Levente and together they walked down the 600 halls to the cafeteria. By the time they got there, lunch was almost over and the usual was going on like every other day: Ben and Allison were fighting over something; Jeremy, trying to figure a way to get a problem wrong; Amy, figuring out a new dance step; Nick B., staring out into space with his mouth full; and so on.

Levente sat down but first bought milk. "I wish I could get at least one bad grade this year," said Levente.

"What? Are you crazy?!" yelled Luke.

"I wish," said Levente.

"You're getting perfect grades. What are you talking about?" asked Luke.

"You wouldn't be saying that if you were experiencing what I am, or have been," said Levente.

Luke and Levente ate their lunch without Jeremy because he was the lunch monitor. The bell rang and lunch was over. They walked back to the room in half an hour. For the rest of the day, Levente got everything correct and completed as usual.

That night at least, Levente wasn't mad because of what grades he got. He was too busy studying his plans on how to get one problem wrong. "$5 \times 5 = 25$. No, that's correct," he said to himself angrily. "Try a more challenging one.

$9 \times 22.5 = 202.5$," he said aloud. "No, that's still right." He was angry. Levente tried over and over, as every day, but it never came. Suddenly, out of nowhere, he shouted, "$4 \times 4 = 15$! I got it! I got it!"

"Are you all right, Levente?" asked his mom.

"No! I'm just so happy!" he kept saying over and over again.

That night he even dreamt about getting answers wrong, but that was not unusual because he dreamt that every day or night ever since kindergarten.

The next morning, Levente went into the classroom happily. Everybody was just staring at him because he had a huge smile from ear to ear and they had never seen him that happy before.

"What's up?" asked John C. and John B. at the same time.

"Oh, you'll see!" said Levente.

"What a weirdo," said the girls as he passed them for the first period. Levente zoomed in and out of Home Ec, finished choir, and went swimming. He demonstrated the frog kick and breaststroke. Math came next, and Mrs. Carlson said, "O.K., class, let's hear what 4×4 equals—Levente?" Levente beamed. HE WAS GOING TO GET A PROBLEM WRONG!!! He shook all over.

"Levente?" Mrs. Carlson asked again.

"16," said Levente.

FANG

by
Becky Jantz

*To Susan Butcher, who inspired me,
and to Keno, my own canine companion*

Chapter One
The Blind Pup

On a cold, wintery Christmas morning, Shay gave birth to a single blind Husky. It needed help —a companion. But the owners were mean and didn't want a blind pup. They decided to send it to the dog pound to be put to sleep.

In the pound, before the blind pup arrived, a family with a little son about four years old were looking for a good companion dog. The parents had their hearts set on a young golden retriever. The boy, Jacob, however, didn't feel a good relationship between the dog and himself. Just then, a young man holding a blind pup entered the pound. Jacob tugged at his mother's dress and said, "That's the doggie I want."

His parents walked over to the man. "Where are you taking this dog?" asked Jacob's mother.

The man, not much older than twenty, said, "We're putting this pup to sleep."

"But my son, Jacob, here wants it and I'm not leaving this pound until he gets it!" exclaimed Jacob's mother.

"Irene, control yourself!" Jacob's father shook her. He looked at the man. "Why are you puttin' this fine pup to sleep?"

"Sir," said the man, "I was given strict orders to put this dog to sleep."

"But why?" asked Jacob.

The man knelt beside Jacob. "Son, this dog is blind."

Jacob was confused. "What's blind mean, Mommy?"

"Honey," said Jacob's mother soothingly, "this man is trying to tell you that the doggie can't see."

The man said, "Sorry," and walked away.

Irene ran in front of the man and stopped him. "We'll buy the pup. How much do you want for him? Is fifty dollars enough? Oh, please, that's all the money I have in my wallet."

"I'll tell you what," said the man. "You can have him for free. There's no point wasting your money on a poor pup like this." And he walked away, leaving a leash and a collar with the pup.

Jacob named him Fang.

Four years passed by and Jacob gave much love to Fang. And even though Fang couldn't see, his strength, sense of direction, and determination showed him the way. Often he would trip and stumble, but he was determined to be a normal dog.

Chapter Two
The Big Storm

One warm, bright sunny day, Jacob and Fang were swimming in the river next to their house. Suddenly, dark clouds formed and covered the sun. A streak of lightning lit up the sky. Then thunder, sounding as loud and as angry as a volcano erupting, shook the whole earth. The waves in the river became big and the current strong.

Jacob swam to the edge of the river and plopped down on the soft, wet ground, breathless. After a few moments, Jacob started pleading to Fang to get out of the rushing river. Fang swam to the edge of the river just as the current swept him back into the rapids. Jacob screamed in terror as he ran along the bank after Fang. Suddenly he tripped and fell. Off went Fang, yelping, not knowing what was happening.

Chapter Three
Is There Any Hope?

Jacob wouldn't eat sometimes; he just picked at his food with the fork. He tried to force his tears to stay in his eyes, but they were so strong that they spilled over his eyelids and onto his cheeks. He would sleep but have terrible nightmares of Fang in the river. He knew Fang was dead.

One night he dreamt about when he first got Fang. The pup was so young and frightened, just all alone in that small black world of his. Jacob remembered how Fang and he became best friends. While Jacob was asleep, tears deeper than ever before came pouring upon his cheeks.

His parents weren't worried. They knew that all of these signs were just the sadness from the loss of Fang.

Henry, Jacob's father, came to Jacob's bed one night and said to him, "Don't give up hope, son. There's still a chance that Fang's alive." And then he left Jacob's room.

Chapter Four
The Search

After a few days, when the storm stopped, the search for Fang began. A small group of men, including Jacob's father and Jacob, were going. They were taking three of the men's Jeeps. Jacob's mother fixed lunches with ham sandwiches, red apples, chips, apple juice, and her famous oatmeal cookies. At 7:15 in the morning, they were off.

Two hours passed by slowly. They didn't find or hear or see anything for a long time. Then, around lunchtime, somebody heard a movement in the underbrush—some kind of animal. It was panting very hard and was making soft, blurry yelps. Its hooves or paws—whatever they were—stopped, and it made a plop, as though it fell down. The men got up very cautiously and peeked through the trees. It was a wolf, they thought. One of the

men picked up his rifle and aimed it at the wolf. His finger touched the trigger and started to pull back slowly, slowly . . .

Jacob screamed, "That's Fang!" and pushed the man over just as the bullet went off and shot into the tree above Fang.

Jacob ran over to Fang and flopped down by his head. "I'm here, Fang! You're all right now! You're gonna be okay! Please, Fang, just give me a sign that you're all right!" He kept stroking Fang's head, but his best friend remained still.

"Get some food and water!" yelled Jacob. Three of the men brought their sandwiches to Fang. Jacob tore them apart and put a piece of ham by Fang, but all he did was breathe very heavily with his long tongue hanging out.

"Where's the water?" demanded Jacob. One of the men drained some apple juice into a cup he had and brought it over to Fang and put it by his head. Jacob forced Fang to drink some, but he was too exhausted to move. Jacob picked up the cup and poured some juice down Fang's dry throat. He swallowed and moved a little. Jacob gave Fang some more apple juice and again he gradually drank it. Finally, after 10 minutes, Fang regained enough strength to drink from the cup by himself.

Jacob gave Fang the rest of the torn sandwiches. He hungrily ate them. Jacob's dad came over to Fang and patted him on the head. "I brought you one of Irene's famous oatmeal cookies. I know it will give you all of your strength back. You know, Fang, you're my favorite dog. I gave all my other dogs just one-half of a cookie. But you're a good dog." He gave Fang the cookie and then walked away.

Chapter Five
Having Fun

All of the men except Henry and Jacob hopped in two of the Jeeps and drove off. Henry lifted Fang into the third Jeep and put him next to Jacob. Henry got in the driver's seat and drove home. When they arrived, Irene was very surprised.

They quickly got Fang's dog bowl and gave him a big pile of dog food and Milk Bones mixed together. Fang lay down beside his bowl and began to eat. In no time at all, he was finished with his lunch.

In the next few days Fang and Jacob took walks by the river. Fang didn't like that very much and Jacob knew it. But when they went in the meadow, far away from the river, Fang became lively. They would chase each other and then trip on purpose and roll down the small hills. But the most fun of all was sliding down the haystacks. They would climb to the top of the stacks and then slide down together and land in the big, soft pile of hay at the bottom.

As the summer passed, they did pretty much the same thing.

One day, Jacob was sitting by the bottom of a haystack when Fang got up and climbed to the top of it. Then he slid down and landed right next to Jacob.

Jacob turned, and they looked at each other right in the eyes. It was almost as though Fang could see him. And, for the first time, Jacob saw Fang give him a big, proud grin.

OH, ANNIE

by
Brooke Homyak

To my family

Marie Crumpet gave a quick glance around the school yard. She was keeping an eye out for her little sister. Annie had a reputation for embarrassing Marie. She didn't want it to happen again. Marie and her friend Amy were talking when Annie darted by. "Hi, Mar," yelled Annie.

"Oh no," Amy whispered to Marie. Annie stopped and jumped on Marie. "Ugh," yelled Marie, "get off!" She managed to pry Annie off her waist.

"My teacher wants to see you, Mar," said Annie.

Annie took Marie's hand as they headed for the building. Marie walked into Annie's classroom. A few teachers were eating lunch at a gathering of desks. Annie's teacher, Mrs. Larth, stood up and walked toward them.

"Marie, I've been waiting for you." She pulled up two chairs next to her desk and told the girls to be seated. Mrs. Larth began, "Annie likes to fool around in class. I think she needs a good example. I talked to your parents and teacher, and I've arranged for Annie to spend a week in your class. Maybe she'll learn the proper way to behave in school."

Marie's face turned red with anger, Annie's pink with joy. Marie was glad when the final bell rang.

The next morning around five o'clock something heavy whacked Marie on the head. "What?" said Marie. She opened one eye. Standing next to her was Annie.

"Oh, I want to kill you," said Marie. "It's five o'clock in the morning."

"I know," said Annie, "but I can't wait to see your class."

"Don't remind me," groaned Marie. "Go back to bed."

"I can't," said Annie. "I'm dressed."

"Well, get in bed with your clothes on then."

"Can't," said Annie.

Marie was getting frustrated with this little game. "Then get in bed with me," said Marie. Annie squeezed into bed with Marie.

At seven o'clock Marie's alarm buzzed. She reached and shut if off. She climbed out of bed and got dressed. Annie was downstairs watching TV. Marie went downstairs and edged into her chair. Annie ran for the table. Mom called for Dad. Mom gave each of them a slice of melon to start. Annie stuck her tongue in the melon and licked. Marie wasn't looking forward to school that day.

Marie and Annie met Amy at the corner of Broad Street and Elm. They walked to school together. When they reached school, the first bell rang.

"Good luck, Mar," said Amy.

"Thanks, Amy, I'm going to need it!"

Annie stood up tall and proud as she walked into Marie's class. Marie hoped no one would notice Annie, but they did. Soon a group of kids were gathered around Annie.

"Isn't she darling?" asked one of the girls.

"Yes," said Annie, and everyone laughed.

Soon the teacher walked in. "Class," she said, "I'd like you to meet Annie Crumpet." Everyone looked at Marie. Marie looked at the floor.

"Annie, please pull up a chair next to Marie's desk," said the teacher. Before long Annie was seated.

"Now," began the teacher, "this is social studies period."

"I know what that is," yelled Annie. She ran to her bookbag and pulled out a social studies textbook. "Look," she said.

"What a big girl," cooed the teacher.

"I can read, too," said Annie. No one heard. Marie was glad.

When the lunch bell rang, everyone bustled around the classroom.

"I'm starved," growled Annie.

"Why don't you go sit with your friends?" asked Marie.

"No," said Annie.

Annie liked to pack her own lunch. Marie watched Annie take out a peanut butter and marshmallow sandwich, a pickle, a lollipop, and a package of jelly beans. Marie looked in her own lunch bag. She saw a soggy salad (from last night's dinner), a little celery, and a few cookies. Marie took out her fork and poked at the salad.

"You should pack your own lunch, Mar," said Annie. Annie was biting into the sandwich; filling was oozing out.

Amy came by carrying a lunch tray. "Amy, over here," called Marie. Amy took a seat next to Marie.

"What's for lunch, Amy?" asked Marie.

"Pizza," said Amy. Marie wished she had bought lunch.

On the way home from school, Marie stopped to buy bread.

"Can I have a soda?" asked Annie.

Marie looked in her wallet. "No," Marie said.

"How about a candy bar?"

"Oh, all right, pick one out."

Of course she picked the most expensive one.

"Oh, Annie," growled Marie, "what am I going to do with you?"

When they got home, their parents were watching the news. It said that a little girl Annie's age was killed in a fire that afternoon.

All of a sudden, Marie realized how much she loved Annie. She went over and hugged Annie. Annie just hugged back!

THE DOG WHO COULD TALK

by
Stacy Whetzel

"Mom, I hear some scratching at the door!" Stacy said curiously. "I'll get it. Wow! Mom, it's a dog and it doesn't have a tag. Can we keep him, please?"

"Well, let me take a look," Mom said.

Stacy was so excited. "Well, can we?" she said.

"I guess so," Mom said, not too happily.

"Come on, Bud," said Stacy.

"Bud?" Mom said. "This dog is female."

"Well, I would still like to call her Bud. Let's go play house, Bud. You can be the baby."

"Yuck," someone said.

"Who said yuck?" Stacy asked.

"I did," Bud said.

"Bud, you said that?" Stacy was astonished!

"Yeah," Bud answered.

"But dogs can't talk!" Stacy said.

"Well, I can."

"No, you can't!"

"Yes, I can."

"But how?" Stacy asked.

By now Stacy was quite shocked. Bud was just

sitting there staring at Stacy. Stacy started to go down the stairs very slowly and quietly. She tried to yell to her mom but she couldn't talk. Bud started to bark for some reason. Stacy went into the kitchen where her mother was. Stacy said, "Mom, Bud talks."

"Don't be silly, Stacy," Mom said.

"I am not being silly, Mom," Stacy said.

Stacy's mom was thinking that Stacy was going nuts. "Are you feeling well, Stacy?" Mom asked.

"Of course not," Stacy said. "Come and see."

"Okay."

Stacy and her mom started up the stairs. They went up two flights of steps. At the top they went into Stacy's room. Then Bud said, "Hi, Mom, what's up?"

Stacy's mom screamed so loud that it felt like the house was going to fall down. "Mom, don't scream!" Stacy said loudly.

"That animal talked to me!"

"Yes, Mom, I told you but you didn't believe me," Stacy said. "Can we still keep her?"

"Of course we can."

"Oh, goody gumdrops! Can I take her to school for Show and Tell?" Stacy asked.

"Maybe," Mom said. Stacy made a bed for Bud right on her bed.

Five years later . . .

"Mom, I am so happy that Bud had puppies."

"Yes, so am I," Mom said happily.

"Mama, Mama, Mama," cried all the puppies.

THE END

FRIENDS—WHO NEEDS THEM???

by
Brenda Diaz

*For Mom and Ellen Brown,
with all my love*

1

Friends—who needs them? To talk, laugh, and tell secrets with. Look at all the friends talking. Together they are happy. With each other. Here I am, all alone and sad.

2

Friends—they eat lunch together. I don't need them. Here I am, eating only my lunch. A ham and cheese sandwich. I talk to it but it does not talk back. I have my sandwich. I don't need friends.

3

Friends—in class they pass notes to each other. The only thing they pass to me is my homework. One more thing they pass to me is my test.

4

After school they play in the playground. With each other. I just sit on the swing and swing, while they run around playing ball together. I am all alone. One more bad thing happened to me. The swing broke. They were laughing at me. I started to cry.

5

I ran all the way home crying. When I got home my mom asked what was wrong. I told her the whole story. I told her everything that happened on the playground. She wiped my tears off. Then she said, "Go upstairs and get ready for dinner." I said, "O.K."

6

The next day after school I went swimming at the swimming pool. The friends were all there. They all were throwing water at each other. I was at the corner of the pool by myself.

7

Then I saw a girl at the other end of the pool. She did not have a friend. Just then her friend showed up. I got tired.

8

So I went home. I went up to my room and asked myself a question. "Friends—who needs them?" I said. I knew the answer. I do.

9

So I decided that from that day forward it was up to me to be a friend. Also, to make some friends.

REX AND THE ROAD

by
Schuyler Merker Pisha

To Jim Henson and Harvey Schuster

Rex

Rex sat in the office, waiting for his punishment. A tall, stern-looking man entered the room. The man wore a red necktie and a grey sport coat. The boy could almost see a long leather whip in the principal's hands. "Did you or did you not throw an eraser at Ms. Hinkleforn?" The man's voice rang out.

"I didn't throw anything," replied Rex. "I just had the eraser on one end of my ruler and the other end off my desk and I, kinda, well, hit the end that wasn't on the desk."

"You know what I meant!" shouted the principal. Rex spent the rest of the day in the office.

Rex walked home from school that day and thought about the things that were happening lately. He was 13 years old, a little on the chubby side, had no friends, and didn't do well in school.

When Rex finally got home, he sat down on the couch with some chocolate cake and watched his favorite TV shows, "The Alien Pie Fighters" and then "Radioactive Killer Wasps." He thought more and more about school and his life in general. He soon came to the conclusion that he would run away from home. Not to be mean to his parents but just to have some time alone.

Rex went up to his room to pack. First he took all the papers and books out of his schoolbag. Then he threw in a box of cookies, six Double Goober chocolate nut flavored candy bars, 37 dollars and 25 cents (his complete savings), four changes of clothes, his raincoat, his red toothbrush, and a tube of minty toothpaste. He hurried to get out of the house before his mother came home from her job at the Sho La May Restaurant.

Rex Leaves Home

Just as Rex stepped out of his house he saw his mother's dark-green Ford pulling into the driveway. For a boy his size he ran awfully fast, and in less than a minute he had turned the corner and was running down 23rd Street.

Rex hadn't really thought over what he would do when he ran away and he was feeling kind of foolish. He walked down to a park and watched two Little League teams play each other. Rex did not know how to play baseball and so was not as amused as he might have been, but still he enjoyed watching the game. It was getting late. Rex looked at his watch; it was dinnertime. He took the cookies out of his bag and ate about half of them for supper.

After dinner Rex was tired, so he lay down on a

bench and tried to sleep. It was very hard because Rex had no pillow or blanket. He put his bag under his head and his raincoat over him and eventually fell asleep.

Hookey

Rex awoke to the sound of a school bell. It was not his school's but a different one, a louder one.

Rex thought. He knew he wasn't going to school but he also couldn't stay out in the open. The grown-ups would question him about going to school. Rex ate two candy bars for breakfast, and puzzled over this. He could hide in the woods if there were any. He could try to blend into a classroom activity at some school but that wouldn't be fun. Then he thought up a good one. He could just pretend to be sick, and he would cough or sneeze if he saw any grown-ups. If they asked him why he was up and around, he could say his doctor told him to get lots of exercise.

He still did not know what to do. He decided to go to a movie. He had heard that "Invasion of the Blue Bunnies From Planet X III" was playing and he was anxious to see it. He went to the nearest theater. It was pretty crowded and there was a long line for the early show. Many adults eyed him strangely so he coughed and sneezed. They still stared but did not speak. When he got to the front of the line, he found that the man behind the counter would not let him in during school hours.

He went to a different theater where they didn't care, watched the movie and enjoyed it very much.

He was hungry so he ate the remaining candy bars and a few cookies. He found a park where kids were having recess and joined them in their games.

Then he went back to the park where he had slept and took a nap. He was awakened by a *slushity-slush-sluck* sound. He looked up and saw a boy about his age riding a scooter through the wet grass near his head. The boy asked him if he had seen a hound dog named Rover come by. Rex said no, but as the boy left Rex asked him if he could come to help him find his dog, and the boy said, "OK."

Chester and His Dog

The boy said that his name was Chester. They came to a big house. Rex saw a tail disappear behind it. "Hey, Chester," said Rex. "I think I saw your dog behind that house. Chester dropped his scooter and ran behind the house. With a leap that was quite amazing to Rex, the boy caught the dog.

Rex and Chester decided to go back to Chester's house. Once they got to the old grey building and inside, they found it was pretty boring. "Rex," Chester said, "let's go to your house." "Nah," said Rex. "It's twice as boring and, er, well, I'm not allowed to have anybody over when my parents are at work." Chester looked at Rex and opened his mouth to say something but decided not to. Rex glanced at his watch. "Oh shoot, I have to get home."

When Rex got back to the park it was almost dark. He decided to get some paper to write a note to his mother. So he went to a store, got paper and pencil and wrote this letter:

Dear Mom,
   I am ok. As you might have guessed I ran away. I'll be back soon. I didn't run away because I was mad at you, I just needed some time alone that's all. I love you and I'll see you soon.

                              Love,
                              Rex

Then he finished off the cookies. He figured he would have to buy more food tomorrow. Then he brushed his teeth and went to bed, this time with more ease.

A New Day

Rex woke up hungry. He decided to go to a corner store near his house and drop off his mother's note on the way. Luckily, it was Saturday and he didn't have to play sick. He dropped off the note and then arrived at Zak's Store. He bought five large bags of chips, ate half of one for breakfast, put the others in his bag, and went off to Chester's house.

When he arrived, Chester was waiting on the steps for him. They decided to go play basketball. They played until lunchtime and Rex won. Then

Chester went home to eat and Rex ate another bag of chips. Chester had to go somewhere with his father so Rex had to do something by himself. He bought some "Sewage Treatment Man" comics and read them over and over again until dinnertime. Then he ate two bags of chips and went to sleep.

Homeward Bound

Rex had planned on going home that day so he decided to leave right after lunch. For breakfast he ate half a bag of chips. Then he decided to take a walk around on his last day. He walked around until he came to the front of the Samuel Z. Lampfrost Memorial Library. He didn't often go to the library to take out books, although he had a card. He thought he might learn a little before school, and reading was one of his OK subjects. He walked in and took out a book about the Revolutionary War. The librarian let him take it out even though he did not have his card with him.

He went back to the old park and read until about two o'clock. Then he ate lunch (chips) and started the walk home. He wanted to get home but he also enjoyed his time away from his house. When he got home he slowly pressed the doorbell.

His mother opened the door and, with a squeal of excitement and joy, hugged her son. When she finally let go she had a long talk about his time on the streets and Rex promised he would never do it again. Then Rex called up Chester and explained the whole thing. He had a big dinner, and then went to bed.

Back to School

The next day Rex went back to school. He did not have to be spoken to once by his teacher and even made a friend named George. George was short and wore glasses. When he got home he, George, and Chester all played basketball.

THE END

JUST A GUY ON A FIELD

by
Kevin Crook

*To my wonderful 6th-grade
teacher, Phoebe Tanner*

Bill just found himself sitting there on a grass field. He didn't know how he got there or why.

There was no wind, he noticed as he sat on the field, and the sky was just a blank white. Bill decided to get up and look around, but it was then he found he couldn't move. He was paralyzed from the neck down but he could move his head.

Bill was now very scared and he opened his mouth to yell for help, but no sound came out.

As he sat there, another thing happened. It happened very quickly. A big pink object came at him. Bill tried to scream but again no noise. The pink thing came and started scrubbing at Bill's legs. He felt a sharp pain, but there was nothing he could do. He looked to see what happened to his legs, but when he looked, his legs weren't there, just pink particles.

Then there was a big gust of wind; nothing was blown away except for the pink things.

And then, in the distance, Bill saw a grey object. It seemed to be coming at him. Nothing at all he could do, just sit there and watch the grey thing come closer and closer. It was now going very fast and it was very close, coming straight for Bill. He closed his eyes because he thought it would hit him. He had his eyes closed for a very long time, and decided finally to open them, very slowly. He did, and when he looked around he noticed he was no longer sitting but standing, and his legs were back.

Then there was a large rumble, and then a crackle; everything around him started to crumple and bunch up, and then Bill was crushed.

Paul was still crumpling the paper when his friend came by.

"What was that a drawing of?" his friend asked.

"Just a stupid picture of a guy on a grassy field," Paul replied.

Then he threw it away.

THE COMPUTER AND THE MOUSE

by
Miranda Beames

*To my family for all their support—Mom, Dad,
Brannon, Jarom, Isaac, Camas, and Jarvis*

It was around the beginning of school.

My best friend, Katie; Joe; and I were all running for class president.

Katie got a camera for her birthday. She was taking pictures of all of us who were running for class president. She said she was going to put them in her yearbook.

Katie's dad got a computer with a mouse for Christmas. She said, "You can do a lot of fun things with it."

Katie is editor of the eighth-grade newspaper.

After Katie went home, she took the pictures she had taken of us and put them into the computer. She used the mouse to change the way the pictures looked.

She was going to try and get us to drop out of running for class president.

Joe is really good at sports.

Katie showed him a picture of himself holding a football with his pants down and he was wearing a diaper. She told him that if he didn't drop out of running for class president she would put the picture in the eighth-grade newspaper. So he dropped out.

She showed me a picture where I had curlers in my hair and green goopy makeup on. She told me that if I didn't drop out of running for class president it would be put into the newspaper. I didn't drop out because I don't put curlers in my hair and don't wear that kind of makeup. The picture got put into the eighth-grade newspaper.

Katie noticed that our teacher, Mrs. Dundey, was catching on. So Katie took a picture of Mrs. Dundey, and put it into the computer and used the mouse to change it. She changed it so that Mrs. Dundey was wearing a miniskirt and a short shirt. Her hair was messed up.

Katie brought a purse to school one day and in it was a computer disk and some pictures. In science we were working with magnets. One of the magnets fell into Katie's purse. She started screaming, "You ruined my pictures! You ruined them!"

I was wondering why she was screaming. A magnet would only ruin a computer disk, not a picture.

After school the next day I went to Katie's house to play. By the computer was a computer disk. It was labeled "Pictures of Joe, Mrs. Dundey, and Kelly."

I was wondering how my name got on the computer disk. Then I understood. Those were the people she took pictures of.

After school the next day I snuck into her house. I set up the computer, and put in the computer disk.

I worked on the code a few times and figured out what she did.

I saw how she used the mouse on the computer.

I found a picture of Katie and put it into the computer.

I used the mouse to make her look fat in a swimming suit wearing an inner tube. I made her hair stand straight up.

I took the picture to school and had someone put it into the eighth-grade newspaper.

I told the teacher what Katie had been doing.

Mrs. Dundey, Katie, and me went to Katie's house after school.

I showed Mrs. Dundey how she did it.

Katie got grounded for a whole year. She couldn't use the computer or go anywhere.

I got to be class president.

THE END

POETRY
WINNERS

My Grandpa Eli

In memory of my grandfather Eli Goldston

My Grandpa Eli was a mug collector
and his mugs weren't normal.
They had faces of
Goliath and his sword,
a rabbi with his scroll,
and the fortune-teller with her stars.
My dad thought his father,
Eli, was the best man ever,
and even though my dad isn't perfect
he's the best to me,
and I hope this feeling goes on
for generations,
and when I look at mugs
I embrace that
feeling.

JOSHUA ELI GOLDSTON

Me and My Sisters

To Melanie and Leeann, my younger sisters

 Every day
Me and my sisters try
To net butterflies.

Day after day
Me and my sisters draw
Yin yang signs.

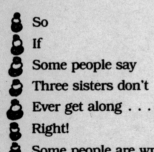 So
If
Some people say
Three sisters don't
Ever get along . . .
Right!
Some people are wrong.

MARIE ANGELINA PAMFILIS

Green Is Money and Grass and Gentle

Green is money and grass and gentle.
Green is the taste of mouthwash.
Seaweed and hair spray smell green.
Envy makes me feel green.
Green is the sound of quiet caterpillars
  and rushing water.
Green is a garden, a bank, and a swamp.
Writing is green. Reading is green.
Green is quiet.

SCOT ROUSSE

New World

Clusters of unknown countries
in a world surrounded by
dust and cobwebs.

Mountains of different sizes
are the only horizon,
except for a hole, a door
to the next dimension—
    clean.

As a giant I walk through
a strangely familiar land,
destroying whole countries
in my path.

I head for the largest mountain,
sit upon the tableland
surveying the damage I have
    caused . . .

until
my mom says,

"Erin, Clean Your Room!"

ERIN ELIZABETH REEVES

A Child's World

To parents—like my parents—
who help to make a better world

Sing a song of wishes, fantasies, and dreams;
Sing a song of make-believe, and rainbow-
  colored streams;
Sing a song of fairy tales, laughter, and joy;
Sing a song of happiness in every girl and boy.

See a scene of runaways freezing in the cold;
See a scene of homeless young, not only old;
See a scene of children starving today;
See a scene of sadness in every lonely day.

Tell a tale of hope, caring, and giving;
Tell a tale of sick children getting well and
  living;
Tell a tale of stopping this world's young sorrow;
Tell a tale of making a happy tomorrow.

STEPHANIE SUTTLE

Basketball

*These poems are dedicated to
my teacher Miss Neal, who inspired me*

Alas, if I weren't so very small,
I'd take that orange basketball
and, flying through the air so thin,
slide it over the top of the rim
and jam it into the waiting net
and score at least two points, I bet!
With the basketball.
If I was tall.
That's all.

Super Bowl

Outside it's snowing,
but inside it's warm.
The fire is glowing.
The TV is on.
Montana is throwing—
a long touchdown bomb.
Rice snares with a fantastic leap.
The snow and ice
outside seem like a dream.
But in here it's cozy and nice.
And there, on our large 27-inch screen,
we watch every play at least twice.
It's the greatest Super Bowl we've ever seen.
And Dad's on the sofa asleep.

ANTHONY FARANDA-DIEDRICH

Silent Moment at the Stick

What a beautiful day.
Tuesday, 5:04 p.m.,
October 17, 1989.

Quiet on the Bay Bridge.
Loud at Candlestick Park.

All of a sudden . . .
   a shake.

Candlestick goes quiet.
Bay Bridge goes loud.

ERNIE VARGAS

Rules

*To my mother, and to my
fourth-grade teacher, Mrs. Kappy Cannon*

Rules, Rules—
  you got to obey.
I went to the principal's
  yesterday.
I was so scared,
  then I realized
    that I got suspended
      right before my eyes.

I was scared, like I said;
I was sad too.
Then another boy came in—
  Guess who?
    He was black.
    He was kicking and screaming,
      but all of a sudden,
        he sat down dreaming.
          He just sat there looking
            into my eyes.

Then all of a sudden I realized
  Maybe he was scared just like me.
    Maybe he was sad.
Then as the time passed,
  he seemed to be glad he came.
    He started pulling at his socks,
      and getting strings.
        He flicked them at the principal's things.

Then she gave us both notes to give
  to our parents when we got home.
"We have a conference on Tuesday,"
  my mom said.
She was nervous all the way.
I know I am in trouble,
  but still I have to move on the double.
    I got to straighten up in school.
      I got to bring in my work and
        stop acting cool.

I don't take the bus and I
  bring in no homework.
    I come into school like some kind
      of jerk.
        I act like I am cool, but I am really
          not.
            I wish I was good and didn't fight.
I know I can be good, if I just try.

And I wonder how that other boy felt,
  that I pushed in the bathroom.
    Maybe he was scared,
      Maybe he was scared just like me.

TRAVIS C. STAFFORD

The "D" Word

To all children of divorced parents

Divorce is the color of black at the midnight
hour.
It sounds like the screech of fingernails on a
chalkboard.
It tastes like the worst sour lemon you have ever
had.
It smells like a burnt rotten pumpkin on your
porch.
Divorce looks like a compacted car at a
junkyard.
It feels like you were dropped and there is no
bottom,
so you will fall and

        fall and

           fall.

MATT BONAFEDE

She Simply Did Not Move

To Mom, Dad and Byron,
with thanks for your support

Mrs. Rosa Parks was very good.
We should remember her, that we should,
Because she did not move!

Rosa Parks was tired that day.
She held her ground and said she'd stay,
Because she would not move!

On December 1, 1955,
The Blacks began to come alive,
Because she did not move!

She got on the bus and took a seat,
Knowing the hurt that she would meet
Because she would not move!

They took her off the city bus,
Not knowing this would cause a fuss,
Because she would not move!

All the while she was in jail,
They were sending special mail,
Because she did not move!

Don't ride the bus said the letter,
Walk instead; that would be better,
Because she did not move!

It only took one woman to show a little light,
To let us know that freedom is worth the fight,
Because she did not move!

Because she did not move!

KIMBERLY COGDELL

New Candle

Our friends gave it to us . . .
a pink, ice candle.

  Pink as a rose,
  tall as a milk carton,
  stretching up
    like a ruler.

The wick
  a plume off a knight's helmet,
  giving off a black ink veil of smoke.

Holes in side, like
  little rooms giving off
    light from inside.

Around the candle wick, a valley,
the wax shrinking as though with fright.

In the center of the table
we fight over who lights
and who blows out, every
night
  at dinner.

JONATHAN G. PACE

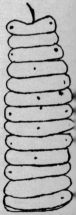

Hair

My mother's black curly hair
        is like
the waves on a dark stormy night.
My father's hair is like a
        silky night.
My brother's hair in the
         morning
         sticks out
         like a
         porcupine.
But my hair is the best
        of all,
    silky, wavy, soft,
     like the color of
       burnt cupcake.

JANE CHOI

To Cats: Three Poems

To my cats, Ida the hunter, Al the night owl,
and good old Shazam

1 Pounce

The cat
crouched,
ready
to pounce,
ready
to kill.
She pounced.
crunch
The leaf
had lost
the battle.

2 Night Eyes

I woke
with a start.
All I could see
was the
big yellow moon
and
two yellow eyes.
I laughed
at myself
for being scared.
My cat
started
to purr.

3 Shazam

My dad
took
my cat
to the vet
and
came back
empty-handed,
and many
nights
I lie
in bed
and cry.

KATHERINE P. MYERS

Stuffed Toys

To all of my family and friends

These cute little toys
are great gifts for girls and boys.
They love to hug them and squeeze them,
and tickle and tease them.

ANGIE BURKE

My Grandfather Tells Me

To my Granddads

My grandfather tells me . . .
I will draw your happiness,
I will find your lost toy,
I will crush your fear into
   a hundred pieces,
I will sing your lullaby,
I will dry your tears.

SARAH ENGLAND

My Dream Girl

To my Mom,
who is always there for me

Her hair is like golden strands of sunlight.
Her eyes are the color of the calm blue sea.
Her voice reminds me of birds in flight.
I hope she likes what reminds her of me.

DANNY COLE

I Am Who I Am

I am who I am, so why should I change?
I love who I am, so why should I change?
I like life the way it is, so why should it change?
I like everything about me, so I don't plan to
   change.

JASON SIESS

I Hear My Day Go By

I hear my alarm clock ringing as I wake up to a
    new day,
I hear my dog whining at my door because she
    always wants to play,
I hear the water running as I brush my teeth
    and wash my face and my sister leaves,
    thinking she is so cool,
I hear my Rice Krispies and then I go to school.

I hear the kids talking when I am there too,
I hear the school bell ringing. I go in and I meet
    you,
I hear my backpack zipper open and my
    homework crackle out,
I hear many voices in my class and, if it gets too
    loud, "Quiet!" the teacher will shout.

I hear many voices in the lunch room,
I hear, when we walk in the hall to go outside,
    the custodian sweeping the floor
    with his broom,
I hear the kids yelling and screaming at recess,
I hear the whistle blow and the playground is
    left lifeless.

I hear the bell again at the end of the day,
I hear the school bus starting, the kids yelling,
    and "Fasten your seat belt please!" the bus
    driver always will say,
I hear Mom greet me as I come home, and I do
    my homework and thirty minutes of reading,
I hear Dad come home and then I'm eating.

I hear Mom telling me it is time to go to bed,
I hear my toothbrush brushing, and I put my
   headgear on, just as my
   orthodontist said.

I hear my sheets going over me
   and then silence.

                              STEFAN LYHNE

ABOUT
THE
AUTHORS

MIRANDA BEAMES, who wrote "The Computer and the Mouse," was born November 12, 1978, in Twin Falls, Idaho, and now lives in Hazelton, Idaho, where she attends Hazelton Elementary School. She has won local awards for her writing and is a serious pianist. She is active in 4-H and enjoys dance, reading, and camping.

☆

MATT BONAFEDE, author of "The 'D' Word," was born in Fullerton, California, May 11, 1978. He lives in Whittier, California, along with his dad, mom, and two brothers, and goes to Granada Middle School. Among his interests are sports, bicycle riding, collecting baseball cards, and drawing.

☆

ANGIE BURKE, the author of "Stuffed Toys," lives in Allison Park, Pennsylvania, and is a student at Central Elementary School. She was born in Orange, California, December 5, 1978. Her interests include drawing, running dashes, basketball, dancing, and learning about ancient Egypt.

☆

JANE CHOI wrote "Hair" when she was a student at Malcolm S. Mackay School in Tenafly, New Jersey, where she still lives and now attends Tenafly Middle School. She was born in Seoul, Korea, May 25, 1979. She likes to ride bikes with her friends and family.

KIMBERLY COGDELL was born June 9, 1978, in Sanford, North Carolina, and goes to Reid Ross Junior High School in Fayetteville, North Carolina, where she lives. "She Simply Did Not Move" was written when she was a student at Edgewood Elementary School, also in Fayetteville. Among her interests are swimming, skating, ballet, writing, and piano.

☆

DANNY COLE wrote "My Dream Girl" as a student at Blaine-Buffalo School in Taylorstown, Pennsylvania. He now attends McGuffey Area Middle School in Claysville, Pennsylvania. He was born June 22, 1977, in Washington, Pennsylvania, where he still lives.

☆

KEVIN CROOK was born in Oakland, California, November 15, 1977. He lives in Berkeley, California, and goes to Martin Luther King Junior High School. He wrote "Just a Guy on a Field" when he was a student at Columbus School in Berkeley. His interests include model trains, volleyball, fencing, basketball, baseball, reading horror books, and watching horror movies.

☆

BRENDA DIAZ wrote "Friends—Who Needs Them???" when she was a student at La Granada Elementary School in Riverside, California, where she lives. She now attends Loma Vista Intermediate School in Riverside. She was born in Corona,

California, August 12, 1978. She likes to read, write, and skate, and hopes to be a poet.

☆

JENNY DUNNING, author of "The Living Doll," was born September 29, 1977, in Onawa, Iowa, and now lives in Decatur, Nebraska, where she attends Lyons-Decatur Northeast School. Besides writing, she enjoys running and swimming.

☆

SARAH ENGLAND, who wrote "My Grandfather Tells Me," lives in Summit, New Jersey, where she is a student at Kent Place School. She was born October 25, 1980, in Winston-Salem, North Carolina. She likes to write, read, draw, and swim.

☆

ANTHONY FARANDA-DIEDRICH was born June 14, 1979, in Lancaster, Pennsylvania, where he still lives and is a student at William E. Nitrauer School. His two poems—"Basketball" and "Super Bowl"—attest to his keen interest in sports.

☆

LEVENTE FULOP lives in Portland, Oregon, and attends H.B. Lee Middle School, the real-life setting for his story "Levente." He was born February 13, 1978, in Hollywood, California. He enjoys reading, soccerball, swimming, and music.

☆

JOSHUA ELI GOLDSTON, the author of "My Grandpa Eli," was born in Princeton, New Jersey, April 2,

1979. He still lives there and goes to Princeton Friends School. Some of his interests are karate, ceramics, Dungeons and Dragons, and humor.

☆

BROOKE HOMYAK, who wrote "Oh, Annie," was born August 12, 1980, in Trenton, New Jersey, and now lives in Hamilton Square, New Jersey, where she attends St. Gregory the Great School. She likes dancing, swimming, soccer, softball, art, and writing.

☆

BECKY JANTZ, the author of "Fang," was born in Fallbrook, California, April 24, 1979. She lives in Temecula, California, and goes to Temecula Elementary School. Writing stories and drawing dogs, horses, and people are among her interests, and she also likes playing softball, biking, taking care of pets, and collecting rocks and shells.

☆

STEFAN LYHNE was born June 27, 1978, in Munich, West Germany. He lives in Coral Springs, Florida, and goes to Coral Springs Middle School. He was a student at Setauket School in Setauket, New York, when he wrote "I Hear My Day Go By." Some of his interests are reading, soccer, tennis, and swimming.

☆

KATHERINE P. MYERS lives in Winnetka, Illinois, and attends Washburne Junior High School. When she wrote "To Cats: Three Poems" she was a student at Samuel Greeley School in Winnetka. She was born December 7, 1978, in Chicago, Illinois. She likes reading, basketball, collecting model horses—and playing with cats.

☆

JONATHAN G. PACE, who wrote "New Candle," was born in Edmonds, Washington, November 8, 1979. He now lives in Chico, California, where he is a student at Marigold Elementary School. His interests include reading, writing, piano, and science, especially astronomy.

☆

MARIE ANGELINA PAMFILIS was born February 16, 1979, in New York City. She lives in Whitethorn, California, and was a student at Whitethorn Elementary School when she wrote "Me and My Sisters." Now she goes to Redway Elementary School in Redway. She likes to write stories and poems and to draw, and she collects business cards.

☆

SCHUYLER MERKER PISHA, the author of "Rex and the Road," was born August 25, 1978, in Sharon, Vermont. He lives in Cambridge, Massachusetts, where he attends Graham and Parks Public Alternative School. Some of his interests are skateboarding, computers, and photography.

☆

ERIN ELIZABETH REEVES was born March 2, 1978, in Bar Harbor, Maine. She lives in Fairfield, Maine, and goes to Lawrence Junior High School. She wrote "New World" as a student at Lawrence Middle School. She likes to write, draw, paint, and play soccer.

☆

SCOT ROUSSE was born in Los Angeles, California, March 15, 1978. He lives in Valrico, Florida, and attends Turkey Creek Junior High School. He was a student at Progress Village School in Tampa, Florida, at the time he wrote "Green Is Money and Grass and Gentle." Skateboarding, computers, and music are among his interests.

☆

JASON SIESS, who wrote "I Am Who I Am," was born June 2, 1980, in St. Louis, Missouri, and now lives in Fenton, Missouri, and goes to St. Paul School. His interests include soccer, baseball, basketball, piano, reading, and writing.

☆

TRAVIS C. STAFFORD was born in Roanoke, Virginia, September 18, 1978, and wrote "Rules" when he was a student at Raleigh Court School. He now lives in Elgin, South Carolina, and goes to Lugoff-Elgin Middle School in Lugoff. His interests include collecting baseball cards, playing the piano, chess, and working toward becoming an Eagle Scout. He wants to be a baseball player and a writer of fantasy. He hopes to go to Harvard to study writing and photography.

MALATHI SUNDARESAN was born in Toronto, Canada, March 16, 1978. She lives in Pearland, Texas, where she attends Pearland Intermediate School. At the time she wrote "A Dream Come True" she was a student at Jamison Middle School in Pearland. She enjoys swimming, tennis, band, and using a personal computer.

☆

STEPHANIE SUTTLE, the author of "A Child's World," was born October 11, 1977, in Yuba City, California, and now lives in Pearland, Texas, and goes to Jamison Middle School. Among her special interests are dancing and writing.

☆

ERNIE VARGAS was born July 1, 1978, in Redwood City, California, and now lives in Watsonville, California, where he is a student at Rolling Hills Middle School. An earthquake in nearby San Francisco inspired him to write "Silent Moment at the Stick." He enjoys reading and also baseball.

☆

STACY WHETZEL, author of "The Dog Who Could Talk," was born in Peoria, Illinois, October 1, 1979. She lives in Fishers, Indiana, and goes to Fishers Elementary School. She likes animals and enjoys dancing, reading, and swimming.

HONORABLE MENTIONS

The work of these eighty-one young writers received honorable mention in the Young Authors of America Contest:

Bradley Albert, South Salem, NY
Holly Arsenault, Brewer, ME
Christopher Barkley, Ithaca, NY
Tyrone M. Baron, Portland, ME
Martin Bernardi, Berkeley, CA
Neil Castiello, Lynbrook, NY
Hae-In Chung, Drexel Hill, PA
Josh Corbeil, Attleboro, MA
Matt Cotton, Monticello, AR
Katrina Cruz, Fremont, CA
Sara Demanette, Concordia, KS
Melissa Dodson, Merced, CA
Katie Doerr, Flint, MI
Jason Dolezel, Troy, MI
Karen Edwards, Brooklyn, NY
Erica Fenik, Bedford, MA
Natalie Ferenczy, Lancaster, PA
Nicholas A. Firetag, Riverside, CA
Dawn Fowler, Warren, MI
Cason Frei, Santa Clara, UT
Aaron Garrison, Royal Oak, MI
Jessica Gladstone, Cross River, NY
Elizabeth Goodson, Beaumont, TX
Nickolas Ryan Harris, Winnett, MT
Jeffrey Hillstead, Wisconsin Rapids, WI
Brian Huffman, Archbold, OH
Miles Hunsberger, Minneapolis, MN
Angie Hurtado, Yuba City, CA
Meryl Ingis, Tenafly, NJ
Jamie Johnson, Vancouver, WA
Mafo Kamanda, Milwaukee, WI
Carla Kampschmidt, Mason, OH
Larry Kelly, Holyoke, MA
Carrie Laflen, Loveland, OH
David Lees, Attleboro, MA
Jimmy Light, Palm Desert, CA

Justin Logan, Geneva, NY
Annie Maresca, Washington, D.C.
Ryan W. McLarney, Marine City, MI
Dallas McNew, Licking, MO
J. A. Meiburger, Springfield, VA
Crystal Menendez, Pittsfield, ME
Cole Meredith, Madison, WI
Brandon Moak, Mesa, AZ
J. T. Nanasy, Williamston, MI
Brandon Nelson, Troy, MI
Matt Nelson, Ukiah, CA
Cindy Nordstrom, West Taylor Ridge, IL
April Nye, Bel Air, MD
Jaime Orovic, White Plains, NY
Andreas Pape, Granville, OH
Heather Pearn, Brooklyn, NY
Andrew Perell, Great Neck, NY
Reed M. Quinn, Fairport, NY
Diana Reese, Johnson City, TN
Sara Robinson, Newberry, MI
Timothy Schneider, Stuyvesant Falls, NY
Lori Segal, Norwich, CT
Nicholas Phillip Seidner, Palm Desert, CA
Alissa Silverman, Atlanta, GA
Demelza Sjostrom, Riverton, WY
Kris Smith, Stuart, VA
Tammy Smith, Kansas City, MO
Ian Spice, Anchorage, AK
Evan Stancil, Baltimore, MD
Soli Stearns, Fremont, CA
Jesse Steinberg, Worthington, OH
Kate Stephenson, West Lebanon, NH
Alison A. Stine, Mansfield, OH
Luke Thomas, Canal Winchester, OH
Jeff Tipton, Edgewood, NM
Brandon N. Towl, Attleboro, MA
Joe Valenti, Highlands Ranch, CO
Adam Waldman, Baltimore, MD
Chris Walters, Petal, MS
Heidi Wheeler, West Newbury, VT
Shane Wilbert, St. Helens, OR
Saira Willis, Taylor, MO
Matt Wise, Independence, MO
Heather Witte, Lakeland, FL
Daniel A. Yost, Broomfield, CO